Nia

If I Only Knew

C.M. Velazquez

978-1-965552-65-0 (Paperback)

admin@bookwrightshouse.com
☎ (213) 286 6700

Chapter 1

Nia

There lived a young lady named Nia. Nia was 17 years old. She goes to Winslow high school. In the city of beetle bills, Oregon. Nia excels in keeping good grades and was a good daughter to her parents, Mr. and Mrs. Rochelle and Robert Mullins.

Temperatures were in the mid 60's giving way to a cool breeze, a spring like feel. She was sitting in her room gazing out the window and her mind wondered about Robin. She thought of him often and wished she would set her heart on other things. She felt the need to talk and did not know if she could trust her brother, Samuel, who just so happened to be his friend. But, instead, she decided to talk to her sister Tracey. Nia felt talking with her would give her a better objective than if she had talked to her brother Samuel. She also felt that although Tracey was only fourteen years of age, she was wise for her years. And so, she did just that. She walked over to Tracey room lightly tapped on her door. Tracey, yells "come in", as she pulls off her headphone around her neck. Nia whisks over to Tracey, and asked, in a whisper—"can you keep a secret?". "Yeah, what is it", responded, Tracey.

"There's this boy in school and I don't think he even looks my way. But, on second thought, said Nia looking rather perplexed, you know, I think he does look my way, because he smiled back". "So, what about him", interrupted Tracey. "Well, I like him, and I think he likes me too". "And so, what next?" said Tracey almost appeared to rush Nia along.

"Well, I just wanted to tell you I like him and maybe he will ask me to be his girl". "Uh, by the way", said Tracey—"keep waiting. Boys now a days don't even ask a girl out. So, if he asks you out for lunch, then that's a sign he is your boyfriend". "Ah, girl" Nia, was a gasp and was amazed what Tracey had just said. After all, she is much younger than Nia.

"I like his neck tattoo, Tracey," Nia said. It isn't large but, big enough to see", she exclaimed as her eyes widen and she giggled with excitement.

Then Nia clearing her throat ask almost embarrassed ..., "How'd you know that, Tracey?"

"I am in school, and I hear girls talk and when that time comes for me, I know, as well. Oh, and by the way, if he does ask you out for lunch, then he is serious with you". Wow, exclaimed, Nia full of excitement. "I will be coming to you for updated 411 on dating clues". Both laughed out loud. "Okay, Tracey, thanks for listening later".

Chapter 2

School tragedy

Following day, Nia woke up feeling cheerful and relieved that she had finally discussed things with her little sister, Tracey. And as she stared out the window, Nia, thought to herself about her sister, she smiled, said softly "she is wise beyond her years".

Mrs. Mullin was in the kitchen, and you could hear the rattling of pots and silverware. She yelled for each as she called them down for breakfast. Samuel, Nia, and Tracey—breakfast is ready. Come before you're late for school. Just at that moment you hear rushing footsteps clamoring down the stairs and their laughter as they hurry to get to the table.

"Oh, mom thank you," said Samuel. 'Yeah, said Nia and Tracey in Unisom—thank you. You better thank the Lord too, before you eat". Each held their heads down and whispered a prayer.

On her way to school she met up with her friends, Natalie and Sophia. So did your boyfriend talk to you yet ask Natalie. "Yeah, did he" mimic Sophia. "No and when it happens believe me you will both be the first to know. And he is not my boyfriend, yet."

While in class Nia would daydream. When will she be his girl. You can hear Ms. Reed in the background calling for Nia. "Nia, Nia", called Ms. Reed. Just then there was a commotion in the hallway and yelling and screaming. Ms. Reed stopped in her tracks and hushed the class, having them stay seated, as she slowly walked to classroom door. Ms. Reed slowly peeked out from the small glass of the door. When she witnessed loud commotion and students yelling and running. Ms. Reed then witnessed a young man in a black masked holding a gun and yelling at everyone to sit down on the ground as he waved a gun. What Ms. Reed also noticed under the shooter mask was a rose tattoo with an eyeball in middle of the rose. She quickly turned around finger pressed to her lips as she commanded her class to sit quietly. She whispered enough for the class can hear, said, "there is a shooter in the building". "You remembered how you were trained". Sit down quietly. Ms. Reed quickly turned to lock the door and push a chair and a desk as quickly and quietly as she can.

She looked at the class and motioned with her finger to sit quietly and with the show of her hands she motioned, to turn off their phones. They obeyed.

You can hear the panic and whimpering as the mask man yells "everyone quiet or I'll shoot right in your tracks. Ms. Reed turned and looked at her students as they sat on the floor curly with their heads between their knees. She felt the anxiety but was limited to what she could do. She knew she had to stand strong and calm for their sake and hers.

Fortunately, for Ms. Reed, the gunman, didn't glance at her room, something she found odd but was grateful for.

Ms. Reed had a demeanor about her. She was a mere 5'2" reserved and cool when put under pressure. But, tough as nails. She was 47 years old with 1 child and husband and all she could think of was getting alive to her family.

She knew her students needed her, now more than ever. She did not want anything to jeopardize their chances of safety.

"Missed Reed, whispered one of the children,—what's happening" She quickly, mouthed hush, so as not to make any significant sound that will attract the shooter to her room.

Ms. Reed gathers the students in a circle while on the floor and brings them closer into a semicircle. She explained to the students, "the shooter is in the hallway, and I've only seen 1". She asked them to remain quiet and not make a sound. She also reminded them to shut off their cell phones and to turn off the vibrate sound.

As they sat quietly in obedience, she could not help but remind herself there are parents out there who are worried sick and are counting on their children to be alive; and she must muster the courage to uphold that. Afterall, she felt she was their second mother, and this was something she had to accomplish.

5 minutes of chaos and the yelling from the shooter—"Now you follow my directions. Push your phones over to me and keep your hands up". You hear the whimper and sobbing of the children.

She motioned to the students to come around and as they sat in a circle on the floor, she said—"now I know some of you may not believe. But this is a time for prayer". They all bow their heads in sync as Ms. Reed began in prayer.

"Lord, you know we need Your protection now. We asked that You please keep us and the other children who are being held safe— may there not be any one hurt or wounded, everyone whispered, Amen". Ms. Reed finished praying; she noticed each student's faces were a look of relief. She looked up then whispered to herself and said, "God you are real".

Right at this point Ms. Reed phone begins to buzz. She was startled and quieted the phone as though it were a living thing. The children watched in amazement as she stumbled to grab it; but managed to shut it off.

The shooter then asks, "who phone was that?" each student responded not mine".

He looked up heading towards the door that he did not think to look. He was stocky build and measured 5'7" in height with a white sleeve t-shirt, blue denim and multi-color sneakers.

As Ms. Reed pressed her cheek to the door to hear if by chance the shooter had left. You can hear his footsteps coming towards the door. As he got closer, the sirens of the police cars were approaching. At that instant you can hear the patter of running feet, which scared him away. A sigh of relief blurted out of Ms. Reeds chest.

Upon hearing this, Ms. Reed whispered to the class as they stared at her for answers. Her facial expression gave away to what they wanted to hear. "I think he ran off". You then can see in their faces a relief and adulation on each one's faces.

Now, there was silence. But Ms. Reed did not know if the shooter had left the building. Unbeknownst to her the shooter did leave the building.

Now, Ms. Reed knew this was a time to sit and wait until an officer came knocking on the door. In the meantime, she gathered the students around as they sat quietly on the floor. She exclaimed, "now this is a time for prayer, although I know is against school policies, we got to pray". The students in unison agreed and they bow their heads, while Ms. Reed began in prayer, "our father who art in heaven, give us this day our daily bread". Just then there was a knock, and everyone gasped in startlement. Hush, Said Ms. Reed. "no one make a sound" they were quiet as a mouse you could hear a pin drop.

When the officer yelled—"is anyone in there, this is officer Mills and I'm checking each classroom". When she opened the door slowly, officer Mills said, "Ma'am, do you have any students with you?" yes, answered Ms. Reed.

Each student knew how to put their hands up once they were told to do so, ever since having drills often in the school it now became surreal. As each did so one by one and as they walked out of the classroom, they knew to be silent. And as they walked out of the school building each one looked to see if they saw their parents. There were guns drawn and a sea of police cars along with a swarm of parents seeking their child and the terror of fear on their faces said how they felt.

After all was said and done. Nia and the families that were present were informed the shooter had left the building without a trace.

Now Officer Mills spoke to the crowd. "Fortunately, no one was shot or killed, but the shooter is still on the loose and there is no telling who or what was the motive'. Officer Mills continued, speaking to the crowd of parents—"keep your eyes open and be vigilant.' Any suspicion or believe in your gut the person could be the shooter, dial 911". As you all know, from the description given, he is estimated to be 5'7" tall.

Nia and Samuel, both hugged each other as they both knew inside it was a close call. But, once realizing what had just happened, they both quickly pulled away. Taking it in stride they laughed and walked home together side by side.

As the two walked home together, Nia decided this would be a good time to be open to Samuel about her love interest. She figured at this point she felt he could be trusted.

"You know Samuel, there's this friend of yours who I find very interesting', "yeah, who might that be" asked Samuel. "You promise not to let mom and dad know"blurted Nia. "Well, you both hang out and joined the same fencing club', he's about your height", with her two fingers pressed together she playfully says—"maybe a smidge taller". She continued to describe him, "Black hair, slim build. Has a goatee and a red rose on his neck". "Wow, yelled Samuel, you really check him out".

So, "You still don't know"—exclaimed Nia, as she walks backwards facing him so as to see an expression of sort.

"I have many friends who I hang out after school and know a lot from my fencing team". Samuel, becoming annoyed—asked Nia. "Why don't you just give me the name, Nia. After what just happened, I can't think, and this is absurd'. Okay, okay, sounding out of breath Nia said "Well, is Tracey".

He stops suddenly—give Nia a look—as if she was from another planet. He walks and turns towards Nia and says—"Nia I don't know about his guy, he seems a bit off". "Off"—exclaimed Nia, "how?"

"Well, Nia, when he is with us, he always seems to be looking behind as if there's someone trailing him. Then there's the time when us guys are together; he gets a beep on his cell phone. Almost like a code. Then a few seconds later, he tells us boys— "got to go and meet someone".

"But I don't know Nia—He can be a nice fella, though". Nia sounded resolute—simply said, "okay good to know".

"What about the family, do you know anything that I should know?" Nia, now becoming inquisitive. Stopping not far from their homes, she asked him.

"Samuel how are his parents', and do he have any siblings?" Samuel becoming flustered and annoyed at the same time. Not believing what he was hearing after what had just happened to them at the school.

"Look, Nia, I told you he hangs out few moments and leaves. I've only met his parents' a few times; they do not look out of normal, and he does have one sister; I think she's two years younger. Samuel, upon recollection, remarked, "In fact, I believe she attends the same school as Tracey." exclaimed Samuel.

Not being phased at Samuels impressions—Nia simply said, "Okay Samuel, pinky swear". He smirked and when along with the pinky swear.

As they both headed home, both in unison yelled in excitement— "Mom guess what happened at the school today?"

Chapter 3

Love in the air

Following day school was closed, but counselors were available for those who seek to meet with them. There was police presence. It was the only reminder of what had just happened. Then you have Ms. Reed who was happy to oblige any way she can. Knowing Ms. Reed, if you know her, you can see she was shaken, but she managed to come and be a part of the team and talk to her students.

Nia was thinking about the talk she had with her brother Samuel and now she felt she was not sure if she should have mentioned it to him.

Well, just as she thought she might not be bothered, Nia gets a tap on her shoulder. She swiftly turned around and to her amazement was Robin. Nia smiled a big smile. Forgetting the feeling she only had minutes ago. Robin was standing there over her. Robin was usually stylish. Always wears a scarf around his neck, which for those who do get to know him, it has become his signature look. Robin smiled back with his arms leaning up against the wall, leaning over Nia.

"How about you and I go for lunch?" Nia smiled and said "fine, where do we meet?"

We can meet in the lobby, and we go from there instructed Robin. "Okay" stammered Nia as she headed off to her classroom and remembering what her sister Tracey said she whispered "now he's my boyfriend".

Chapter 4

12:00pm

Nia and Robin met at the lobby as agreed twelve o'clock. They decided to go to the fountain diner that was near the school. As they sat, they stared at each other and giggled, enjoying one another's company. Only time they stopped staring was when the waiter came to get their order. Once they put in their orders, they went back to staring and holding each other hands.

So, tell me, Robin said—what took us this long to have lunch—Nia smiled. Robin admittedly said how he always wanted to talk to her but was not sure if Nia was hooked up to someone else.

Robin explains as he held her hands across the table and gazes into Nia eyes, as though looking for answers. He pursed his lips and said—"I had to make sure you were not". And how'd you know I'm not asked Nia?

Well let's say, I know and smiled.

"Well, said Nia I've always wondered if you would be interested in me"—"oh I was exclaimed Robin.

"Hey, is that your brother, Samuel?" "Yeah, that is my brother"—Nia answered unenthused.

"I shoot hoops with him sometimes. He's a cool dude", I like him—Robin said.

Did he tell you about me, Nia blurted out.

No—we don't talk much but, when we do it is about meeting up to play ball. Guy stuff, that's all.

The waitress stops by their table and asks what they will have. Ladies first replied to Robin. I'll have a chocolate shake and fries only. That's all—blurted Nia.

Robin then tells the waitress—"you know add a burger and lemonade, please".

"Sure nuf" replied the waitress and will that be all? both answered "yes" simultaneously and giggled.

Both were enjoying each other's company—smiling, joking as they held hands.

Once the orders came, they wasted no time digging in the food.

"Boy, said Nia we were hungry, huh?'" Robin then looking at his watch realizes he must head back to class.

"Hey, Robin were you near shooting I'm sure you must have heard about it". Robin face became stoic and unsure as what to say.

"What do you think, I was invisible" blurted Robin. "Of course, I've heard I was damn lucky the classroom I was in, was on the opposite side of the shooting".

"Sorry I brought it up, but I only wanted to know if you have heard anything." "Like what Nia", yelled Robin. "I don't know, just word of mouth about the reasons or shooter's identity". Replied Nia.

"No, I did not"—Robin was now annoyed. Wishing Nia would get off the topic. "Well, said Robin, his voice sounded normal not wanting to trigger any suspicion. So, he felt awkward not sure as what to answer, simply said, "I'm just sure glad the shooter did not actually shoot anyone".

"Robin, I did not mean to upset you" explains Nia as she places her hand over his shoulder. "But don't you think it odd that the shooter would just wave his gun, shoot up in the air not purposely to kill or wound anyone. It's just odd".

"I have no idea—maybe keeping score or just for the fun of it" Robin answered becoming annoyed. "What a way to have fun— Nia" said childlike. "Well, when they find him, he'll know what fun is".

"Are we going to see each other again?" asked Robin, sounding impatient. "Does this mean we're dating?" Nia eyes bulged in glee.

Robin poked his finger onto her nose smiled leaned down towards her left side of her cheek and whispered ever so softly "yes my girl" and planted a kiss softly on her lips.

They now arrived at the school and before going their separate ways, Robin then turned to Nia and apologized for getting angry. Robin however felt he had to make it a point in letting Nia know, he had a nice time and hoped she did too. Nia looked up at him, lovingly and agreed she had a nice time as well. She then said to Robin, as though she was scolding a child—"but, don't let it happen again". I won't, said Robin, with a flirtatious smile on his face.

"So, a repeat" he asked. "Sure" Nia answered. We can meet at our usual spot in the lobby. Okay, tomorrow—both agreed.

Chapter 5

Getting to know you

Over time Nia and Robin began to grow closer. Every day without fail they will meet up in the school lobby in the morning before heading to their classes and meet again for lunchtime.

Nia never gave an inkling to her parents that she was dating. She did not feel ready to involve them if this did not go further. She thought and felt this maybe the one but still did not want to let her parents know, yet.

On the weekends Nia would sneak out to meet Robin and meet at the park. Playfully, splash water at each other from the water fountain. To Nia Robin was just a gentleman. But her friends Natalie and Sophia noticed something was odd about Robin.

On their way home from school, they met with Nia. Both Sophia and Natalie had to meet Nia, before she met Robin. For one Natalie and Sophia were not seeing her as much or hardly.

So, the opportunity came. "Nia!" yelled Natalie and Sophia as they saw her heading towards Robin direction.

Nia turned around startled at what was the commotion. "Hey girl said Natalie. 'We don't see you hardly and If you're not running to class, you're running to see him". "Do you have any free time?" Nia, looked down at her watch and replied, "sure in 5 minutes, what's up".

"Whenever you're with Robin does, he ever has outbursts?". Like for example did you ever bring up the time of the shooting did he?" "He has" agreed Nia. Not letting them in on the outburst he just had yesterday.

"But I can understand that was a tragedy that happened", explained Nia. "Yes, it was" chimed Natalie. "I don't know, can't quite pinpoint it but, he's not the one Nia"—said Natalie.

"Hey, Nia" yelled Robin. "Okay ladies I got to go," said Nia. "Later 'said both Natalie and Sophia, "Okay then but, remember what we told you; as both Natalie and Sophia stood by watching as Nia walked over to Robin.

Nia and Robin had made plans to take a walk to the park, not far from the school. It was a warm sunny day. And she felt so free to talk and not to be an enclosed place. She felt happy. So free to talk with no interruptions. So, they thought.

Robin talked about his living in a moderate house with his mom, Ms. Betty Finds. Robin spoke highly of his mother, who was a librarian. She has since retired and has been a stay-at-home mom. His father, Mr. Alvin Finds was a salesman. But his dad was not always home. And when he was, he was never in a good mood. He came home too exhausted to talk or smile. My sister Patricia and I knew not to bother him. Robin said his father would be away for 3 days at a time and would come home and could not understand how his mother would put up with his arrogance. Patricia, she seemed "ok". Nia, he said as he turned to her, my mother was the one that kept the family together. She made it feel like a home.

Robin felt at ease as he could talk with Nia openly. As they walked side by side hand in hand. Nia listened attentively. This was a magic moment for both as they talked almost the whole afternoon. Nia realized she had to get home, because it was getting late and her mom would worry. Robin, we can catch up some more later, is that okay. Okay, as they kissed goodbye. Nia left feeling giddy. As she arrived home, she yelled to her parents'—Mom dad, "I'm home. Okay, dear replied her mother. She ran up to her room, dropped her books to the floor. As she then threw herself on to her bed gazing up at her ceiling with a happy smile. But little did anyone know Robin had a dark side.

Chapter 6

Alpine Diner

Every night between the hour 10pm to 11pm when everyone was sound asleep, Robin would sneak out from his home and meet with his three other friends waiting by the Alpine bar who were already sitting in a booth waiting to begin planning their next stick up.

From afar you can hear the juke box playing the song—"you got to know when to fold them."

Robin thought to himself. Is this song giving him a warning of sort. Hmm, he thought and went along to meet up with the boys. Although Robin knew this was not the way to make money, it was his solution. His quickest way. Having his father away for days at a time, he felt he had to step up and be the bread maker. But faster. Robin thought about his mother and sister.

He worried about his mother. Robin saw it on her face succumbed to worry. Her face said it all. He figured that she might be wondering where she will make ends meet. He worried about her worrying. He knows if his mother knew what he was doing it would make her feel even worse.

One day, Robin overheard his mother talking to his aunt Millicent, about his father staying out more days than Robin had imagined. She heard his mother saying the rents behind and when there was money for the rent there was not much for food. She overheard his mother say to his aunt "I think he is seeing someone", Millicent. He is out and always short of money.

As for Robin he knew better, he knew he can get a decent job but, this so call "job" was going to get things fixed right away or at least until his dad can. Afterall, he felt this will be his last stick up.

The evening was cool. There was a mist in the air and music playing in the background. All the fellas gather around in the corner booth towards the end of the bar. Darryl was the engineer of the plan. He was the older one in the group. Darryl hair was long at times looking unkept. He was brawny, giving the appearance of one who works out. He wore a black and red plaid flannel shirt, looking like a lumber jack. His face was always scruffy as though he hadn't slept and shaved in months. Then there's Keith, young chap. He was youngest in the group. He was scrawny. He had a face of a 19-year-old but was 23 in age.

His parents strung out on drugs, since he can remember. He was taken into foster homes to foster homes. He couldn't stand the bureaucracy of being bounced from home to home. So, he ran away one night and has been on his own since the age of 12 years old. He was now the lookout man thin build, black curly hair. Kenneth was the driver wearing thin wiry glasses, hair slick back as though he had sheen in his hair. Then there's Robin who will attempt to open the safe cracker.

Now, said Darryl we're going tomorrow 10p to the bodega, the one on pine and grove. I've watched the owner who has a safe that is behind the counter. How'd you know this asked Robin. Well, his nephew, Pacheco talks a lot. He brags how his uncle has "mint" you know money and that no one is to know about his hidden safe. His facial expression was of disbelief, Keith blurted—"Darryl, he told you this?". "Well, said Darryl with a smirk on his face, I'm his friend and one who he trusts. 'After all the only reason Pacheco knows, was that the other night his uncle, asked him to watch the front while he goes to the john; and he seen it under the counter".

"Okay, okay, now what' Robin said seemingly annoyed. Well, He usually closes the bar quarter to eleven, when customers are slow and all quiet. That's our chance—got it, boys". Everyone listened attentively; however, Robin sensed something was amiss, although he was now fully committed. He could not back out now. He even thought of the good times with Nia as the fellas were going over the run down.

He remembered his great time with Nia and knew she'd be disappointed to learn he was involved. As he snapped out of his thought he murmured "I'm in now and there was no way to drop out now".

Kenneth told Darryl to keep the motor running. "Keith is to time us—remember—2 minutes flat", said Darryl.

"Darryl gave a weak smile and said, 'Robin, you need to get started on that safe—pun intended.'" And if anything goes wrong everyone split up in different directions, remember".

Hey, yelled Darryl to Robin with a toothpick in his mouth— Darryl now whispers not letting in on the others what he knows. "I watched you and your young lady friend—canoodling' and looks like love"—he said with a sinister smirk on his face. At this point Robin becomes annoyed and looks eye to eye at Darryl. He stands up as though ready to brawl. The other fellows quickly got up from their seats and pulled them apart.

Now, as they walked out of the bar, they gathered around one last time. Darryl reminded them tomorrow at 10pm no sooner or later.

Chapter 7

Moving Forward

Nia and Robin met like clockwork in the lobby and gave each other a quick peck on the lips. They both agreed to meet again at lunchtime. Nia's class was with Ms. Reed, and she felt as though she hadn't been in Ms. Reed class for some time, for her mind was on Robin.

All right class since our last meeting how is everyone doing? The class answered at once. One student shouted, "little shaken up". "I'm alive," said another. "I don't want to be here", said another. And another, "I don't want to be here, but where will I go". Class burst out into laughter.

"All right, all right class, I get it" said Ms. Reed as she clapped her hands attempting to get the class attention. I understand, remember I was here too. But you showed up. And that matters. It shows me how much courage and strength you have within yourselves to move forward. So, I applaud you. As a matter of fact, please I ask each one of you to put your hands together and give yourselves a rounding hand of applause. As you hear the thunderous claps and whistles—Ms. Reed shouts above the clamor—and "in appreciation and making the effort to be here, there will be no homework today". The class clapped and clapped each student looked at each other smiled with approval—until Ms. Reed had to tell them to stop.

"Now, Ms. Reed continued as she caught her breath. 'I want to tell you that that shooter was a coward. He has demons he needs to work out. And remember, just like that we prayed, and poof he vanished". "No one was hurt. Or, traumatized of course. But because we followed instructions stood quiet and prayed the demon left out of here". The class began to laugh. "And It worked!" she shouted above the class laughter". "Do you hear me?"—yes Ms. Reed.

"Now, don't go scooping down to his level just to get someone's attention". The class snickers.

"Another thing I remember, students", said Ms. Reed. 'When I went up to the door and 1 peeked through glass—I seen the shooter". All the students gasped in astonishment. Well not the shooter face. Ms. Reed said in clarity and now having the class's undivided attention you could hear a pin drop.

"I was able to see what the shooter had on. He was a male Caucasian with a red rose and eyeball tattoo on his neck". Remember that key thing so if you see a red rose tattoo let me or principal Harewood know".

Everyone left the class when the dismissal bell rang. Each one thanked Ms. Reed and as they walked out the class appearing bothered at what they have just heard.

Chapter 8

Surprise

After class Nia and Robin met up at the usual spot and walked hand in hand to the park. Robin, however, appeared paranoid after knowing Darryl was watching him. He was not himself. Nia noticed it too. "Robin, are you ok?" "Yes, I am fine"—responded Robin. He then explained that there was something on his mind that he needed to do and that perhaps it's best they meet at another time. "Its Fine", responded Nia.

"Hey, said Nia before they left separate ways. If you like we can meet up tomorrow or we can play it by ear". Both agreed. Robin walked Nia back to the school and each gave a long kiss then said their goodbyes. Nia for some strange reason felt like this would be her last time seeing him. "May, I ask you something else" Nia asked, as she smiled lovingly at him. "Do you always wear scarves, Nia asked as she playfully held the tail end of it. She stared very intently into his eyes; almost as if she was fishing for some answers.

"Is my fashion look", Robin smiled but was a bit surprised at her question. He then stepped back then twirled around as if modeling for her. Robin smiling simply said to Nia, "one day I won't have it on, and I'll surprise you."

As he was walking home Robin ran into Kenneth.

"Hey, bro what was that all about last night. You really got pissed when Darryl said he knows about you and your new "boo".

"Well, I felt what I do outside of what we are planning is none of his business".

"Okay—Robin I didn't mean to rile you up—I just was wondering what ticked you off—said Kenneth. "Well, that is what ticked me off"—Robin responded in anger.

"Now, let us get off the topic"—said Robin obviously annoyed. "I will meet you all tonight".

"All right, alright said Kenneth I hear you, see you tonight".

Chapter 9

Can it be true

Nia looked happy as she headed to class. She met Sophia. "Hey Nia, not sure if you heard—Ms. Reed said she saw the shooter—well not his face but the tattoo he had on his neck. She said it was a red rose and if we see anyone with that tattoo to let her know".

Nia was taken aback and thought to herself as Sophia was going on about the shooter. Ironic she wondered if it could be Robin, nah it's too far-fetch, but gee he is always wearing a scarf—never divulging her thought to Sophia and Natalie.

Once she arrives home, she can smell the food from the door. Nia said her "hello's" to both her parents' who were both in the kitchen preparing dinner. Nia raises her nose in the air, and yells— "mom what your cooking?" smells good.

"Oh, cooking a roast dear." "Ooh smells great" as Nia puts her books down goes give both parents' a kiss. As she was ready to leave, Ms. Mullins yells out loud, "Nia go and wash up and tell your sister and brother dinner be ready in half hour".

Nia stops by Samuels room and knocks softly on the door. Nia hears buzzing sounds as though he was listening to music on his headphones. She walks right in taps Samuel on the shoulder, Samuels was startled—and pulls the headphones off.

"Hey, Nia" Samuel exclaimed seemingly glad to see her, "what's up?" 'But wait before you answer. Did you hear word has it from your two buddies; Sophia and Natalie—Ms. Reed can ID the shooter".

"Yes, I heard they spoke to me about it. Nia, looked to be lost in thought. 'Well, you know I came to talk to you about that to-oh and to tell you, mom said dinner will be ready in half hour".

"Samuel—whispered Nia—'you hang out with Robin. Did you ever seen him act strange?".

"Well, he does not hang out long enough with us to shoot the breeze. But nothing wrong with that." "Wait, what going on Nia?" Samuel became curious.

"No, No I was just wondering. Never mind. We talk later, going to get ready for dinner". Nia then taps on Tracey's door and yells out—"Tracey dinners ready soon". "Okay", yelled back Tracey.

As Nia headed to her room, she plopped down on her bed staring up into the ceiling. She then gathered herself and went down for dinner.

All five gathered at the table said their grace and began to eat their meal. It was quiet at the table all you heard were the clatter of utensils hitting onto the plates. Are you all right, Nia, askes Ms. Mullins. As she added more mashed potatoes onto her plate.

"Oh, I'm fine mom. Just thinking about the homework, I got". Samuel and Tracey gave each other a odd look knowingly it was not that.

Chapter 10

Natalie and Sophia

Next day at school Nia meets Robin. She was not her usual bubbly self. Nia felt withdrawn and nervous, all in one; in hopes that whatever she was thinking was untrue. And she kept this within.

"Hey babe"—Robin yelled getting Nia attention. Robin struts up to Nia with a big smile, happy to see her. He then leans towards her, presses his lips together ready to lock lips. Suddenly, as he got closer to her face, she purposely turned her head so Robin does not kiss her on her lips.

"Hey, hey, what did I do?" blurted Robin. "Look I got to get to class" Nia seemingly nervous, then said abruptly—"we meet later— we got to talk, same place same time" as she ran to her next class.

Sophia and Natalie met Nia. As they walked the halls to class the girls kept silent. Neither ready to speak, until Nia initiated the conversation.

"You know, I'm not sure if I still want to be Robins girl". "Why not?" asked Natalie. 'It's just that I don't think I'm Ready to date. I have lots of schoolwork and trying to keep my grades and dating is a lot' you know".

"I just think we ought to agree and see each other as friends and not as girlfriend and boyfriend. I feel a lot of pressure on top of my schoolwork. She suddenly turns towards both Natalie and Sophia and remarks—"You understand, don't you?"

Both Sophia and Natalie listened as Nia let out her woes. They looked at each other unsure where this was coming from. Or was there something she was hiding from them.

"You sure you want to do this—remarked Sophia—think this through". 'We know how much you could not wait for him to ask you out; now he did and you want to break it off". "Look, Nia,'—said Natalie, is there something else you're not telling us?'. "We would hate to see you regret it later—right Sophia"—asked Natalie. "He will see another girl"—Natalie teased.

Nia gave a big sigh and smiled at the both of them and exclaimed—"shut up you two, I love you both—and thank you" as they gave each other a group hug.

Nia waited in the lobby as they both agreed. She waited and waited and no Robin. She wondered what had happened. Eventually, she stopped waiting and left to go home.

Chapter 11

Is it him?

When Nia arrived home and said her hellos and placed her books down by the foyer. She noticed Samuel who looked as though something he wanted to tell her. He looked anxious as he waited in the living room. "Hello dear—said Ms. Mullins. How was your day today' as she yelled from the kitchen—not bad mom still trying to keep my grades".

"Nia—said Samuel as he called out her name not wanting their mother to know. 'Robin stopped by here earlier. What?" shrieked Nia. As both continued to whisper not letting on to both their parents.

"He said to tell you to forgive him. 'He could not meet with you for fear of what you were going to tell him. He said to forgive him". "what's going Nia", asked Samuel. Samuel continued and said—"I know he is not a talkative person, but you can tell his demeanor—says a lot. 'Since when you became an expert body language person exclaimed Nia", as she slapped her back hand on to his stomach.

"I don't know myself what it is"—Nia said solemnly. "That queasy feeling in the pit of my stomach—not a good vibe I'm getting Samuel. But he must sense something. Reasons how come he did not want to meet".

"Samuel" said Nia—"do you remember when I went to your room and I wanted to talk, but then left?".

Nia looked around her making sure no one was nearby. "You know whispered Nia. Ms. Reed mentioned that she can ID the shooter'. Samuel listened intently as Nia went on …, "Ms. Reed said if you see a red rose with an eyeball tattoo on his neck to inform her and principal Harewood". "Yeah, so"—Samuel sounding dismissive. "Oh, wait' you don't think he is the shooter?'—No way, Nia. Whatever possess you to think such thing?".

"Well, I believe is Robin!" Samuel could not believe what he just heard from his sister; let alone hearing that it could be someone who he nearly sees every day and shoot hoops with, Robin was beyond belief. "I know that he seems strange. But you got to be kidding me", Samuel sounding surprised." "I am not sure" Nia becoming resolute, said, he sounds like one who is" appearing somber.

"Samuel"—said Nia, speaking softly with a concern in her voice. 'Have you ever wondered what's with Robin and wearing of scarfs?" 'I mean they are cute and all and have become his signature look. But can that have been an excuse for him to be wearing does scarfs as a cover up". "Samuel!" exclaimed Nia "think"—with such sternness in her voice.

"You have a point—as he placed his finger on his face giving an appearance as a sleuth detective. You are onto something'. But do you have proof Nia. I mean is a speculation. You are not sure".

Nia seemed perplexed. But she was becoming anxious at the same time. "What if we discover it is Robin after all—," she nervously asked. As both paced back and forth.

"Look Nia"—Samuel sternly said to her. You must stay away from him. We will figure out how to get that scarf pulled off him, just to be sure.

Chapter 12

Overheard

Nia met Natalie on her way to school. Both Natalie and Nia stopped by scoop ice cream parlor. Natalie put in her order, bon bon chocolate and Nia ordered cool mint. As they sat and waited, they talked laughed and reminisced when they used to spend their time together at scoops ice cream parlor while on their school break. Once their ice cream arrived the girls eye widened with delight and began digging in to eat. Just then a student named Jackson came in and to his surprise he noticed the girls and stopped by their booth.

He asked if Nia could excuse herself as he talks with her for a moment. Nia tells Jackson, "It was find whatever you have to say, Natalie can be present' and states matter of fact, "Jackson she been my friend a long time". "Okay, then" said Jackson and he continues.

"Nia what I am about to tell you, has to do with your boyfriend Robin. I was at the bar the night he and his three other friends were planning a heist. "What said Nia in disbelief" "quiet"—said Jackson looking around making sure no one of the boys in the group were around.

"Nia, I know this might be hard for you to hear, but I heard Robin planning a heist with the boys". "I know Jackson you mentioned that already'. "Well, I just thought you should know, being his lady and all". "Well, I'm not now",—Nia said in disgust. Confirming what she had thought all along.

"I've overheard Robin speaking with Kenneth. Kenneth is not from here he is an older person". "What did you hear exactly" asked Nia—seemingly impatient and hoping what she was thinking all along it isn't what she been wondering after all.

Jackson continued…, "then, I heard Robin tell Kenneth that it better go through because this will his last run". Nia face looked perplexed and muttered in her breath—"hmmm".

Nia began to feel a queasy and after talking with her brother and how to solve this she felt now for sure Samuel curiosity was correct. "Are you thinking what I'm thinking"—exclaimed Natalie. Her eyes widened and appeared overly excited. "Should we mention this to Ms. Reed?' "Wait Natalie", "wait for what blurted Natalie— this might be him'. "We can just have him walking around thinking is ok what he did to our school. Or did you forget?'. "Especially to us pretending he is our friend. No correction—more so to you. Lying. He is an imposter, Nia". "So, what's your bright plan" Natalie demanded.

"Honestly, this has been on my mind I haven't met with him for couple of days. You know what, lets' go and tell Ms. Reed". Both got up and left scoop ice cream parlor, anxiously ready to let Ms. Reed know.

Chapter 13

Not real

Meanwhile, Robin meets with Nia as she walks into the school. As he holds out his hands—looking for sympathy he begins to explain reasons he has not seen her in some time. Nia then nods her head to the two to go ahead without her. She stares at him not believing what might be true. She starts to feel uneasy again in the pit of her stomach.

Robin pulls her to the side and whispers—"Nia there's something I have to tell you". Nia thought to herself could she be correct about him. Her hands are becoming sweaty and stomach tight in a knot. "Nia, you don't look ok—are you alright" asks Robin as he holds her shoulders.

"What, I don't know" said Nia not wanting to lead him on she has an idea he is the shooter. Nia fate was now coming to an end. What she dreaded was coming to light. And what she anticipated was making her feel so uneasy. Her world will be over in a few minutes. Hope against hope, but eventually the truth will come out. She felt sweaty and dizzy. Nia fainted.

There was chaos. You can hear the gasp and screams in the halls. Students who now were heading to their perspective classes stopped on their tracks to stop and look. Robin now nervously felt lost. He tried picking her up. Once he saw Ms. Reed heading towards them, he fled.

Natalie and Jackson came running down the hall with Ms. Reed. Ms. Reed came running when she saw what had transpired. Ms. Reed was frantic pushing students out of the way as she managed to get through the mob of students circling Nia.

"Out of the way Ms. Reed yelled, get to your classes, this is not a side show, get to your classes do you hear me—"Nia, Nia" yelled Ms. Reed, slapping her a few times on her face attempting to bring her to consciousness. Nia looked to be coming though—when she softly spoke and said, "am I o.k.?"

"Come with me" said Ms. Reed as she picked her up from the floor. Ms. Reed held her up as they began slowly walking to the nurse's office to oversee Nia condition.

As they arrived to see the school nurse, Mrs. Dubinsky, she then began to check Nia pulse. Ms. Reed softly talked to Nia and asked her, "Nia, I know you may know about Robin, Natalie and Sophia told me".

"Well, remarked Ms. Reed it is time Robin ought to be approached. And this is what I wanted to tell you, Nia. I knew since hearing you two are an item"—Ms. Reed voice became stern and poise and serious. It made Nia feel more nervous. Nia was almost inaudible and shaken said—"but Ms. Reed we were an item, and I haven't seen him for couple of days' The only time was now in the lobby".

In the meantime, assistant principal Jones was making his usual walks through the halls when he saw Nia. "Nia said principal Jones—I've heard what happened to you out in the lobby' Are you ok?"

Mr. Jones asked Nia would she know if Robin will be in school today. He explained to Nia the dire need he needed to speak to him. Principal Jones, Nia said, "He is not in school at all".

Nia looked to be getting her strength back, pushed herself up sitting erect and exclaimed "I don't think he's returning to school again".

"Do you know, where he may go?" asked Principal Jones. No, answered Nia. 'But I do know he has family that lives in Seattle, Washington". "Well, that's a head start. I will call the police precinct informing them". After hearing this Nia began to sob.

Chapter 14

D-day

It is now 9:45pm and Robin has been hiding. Robin was not far from where he had to meet the other three. Robin felt ill in doing such scheme. But he kept his word. He was coming and did not want to go back out. Yet did not want to look like a wimp. Robin thought about Nia and their happier times together.

Why did I get myself into this thought Robin to himself. He began to hit himself on the head in disgust.

Robin watching from a far saw Kenneth pulling up behind the store, then one minute later the other two Darryl and Keith.

Robin was murmuring to himself still not feeling all that great—came out from hiding and went to the bar and appeared to the boys. "Well, gangs all are".

As they congregated and began to review what must be done, little did they know there was an undercover officer Williams who was in the store. He was a 6′1″ muscular, curly dark hair wearing a grey t-shirt and jeans acting as the assistant to the store owner, Mr. Pritchett.

Mr. Pritchett was nervous. Now, Officer Williams walked over to Mr. Pritchett, reviewing where he would be standing so he does not feel he is alone. He then signals to the other two undercover officers, Morgan Ryker and Reagan Sawyer who were sitting in one of the booths. Last minutes checkup were being done, such as the small wire device so the other officers can be notified.

Instant the two strolled in Kenneth and Darryl leaned over the counter and acted as though they were going to make an order when Darryl stood face to face with the clerk and demanded to put his hands up.

He then jumped over the counter pointing the gun at the clerk demanding to show him the safe. As he pointed to the safe, officer Williams leaped at Darryl and grabbed his gun-pointing at it right at Darryl. Watching what was happening Robin did not even have a chance to go over the counter when Officer Ryker and Sawyer ran into action. They grabbed Keith and threw him and Robin on the floor.

From afar Kenneth saw the commotion started to rev up the engine and floor it. Little did he know there was a roadblock. Officers were waiting down the road with their guns drawn.

Kenneth stopped suddenly eyes looked red with fear. You can hear the revving of the motor as Kenneth looked at the officers, and they stared down at him as their guns were drawn. He wiped his eye because they were blurry from the sweat in his brows.

He began to hit his steering wheel with disgust and that feeling of being trapped. Officers were yelling to each other—"we better get out of the way 'he's coming at us". One of the officers stood on his ground and shot right through the windshield; Kenneth was hit. He now had one hand on the steering wheel and one on his shoulder blade. Making Kenneth angry, he revved his car one more time and suddenly went for it and sped through the officers. All you heard were shooting of firearms blaring. Kenneth Car spun out of control, it finally came to a halt sideways.

All the officers came to the vehicle with their guns drawn. They stood and watched as they heard Kenneth groaning as his head bled and chest immersed in blood. In its surroundings you hear the background voices of the walkie talkies from the officers. One yelled for an ambulance.

Darryl, Keith and Robin were each taken into the squad car. One of the arresting officers, officer Gaines noticed the face of one of the male suspects. He also noticed the rose tattoo and eyeball in the middle. He quickly got out of his car and walked to the arresting officer who had Robin in the police vehicle. He spoke with the officer—he then walked over to Robin and in a sarcastic remarked said—"you know you're going to prison big time". "Do you even know what I'm talking about,son?"

Robin's hands were handcuffed to his back and hearing the officer say this, there was nothing he could do but stare. He knew what he did was wrong but he had to do it. Was it worth it, he thought to himself. No, but he had to show the other fellas he wasn't a wimp. He now knew he had lost Nia. He has lost Nia for good.

"We got him!" yelled officer Gaines to the other officers in elation.

In the meantime, there were swarmed of reporters by the precinct, waiting to report on the finding of the shooter now caught in the robbery.

Chapter 15

love lost

Nia was home from school wondering whatever happened to Robin. She felt the missed of his presence.

All the while she knew, knowing what had been said about him, she had to forget him and move on. Realizing this she did feel at ease but wishing she could see him one more time. Nia felt there was some good in him—well she thought so.

Nia gave a big sigh as she sat in her bed. Samuel pushed open the door out of breath yelling—"Nia, Nia did you hear". "No what" responded Nia. Robin was arrested. "Arrested"—exclaimed Nia "for what?".

Samuel now looking as though he had run a marathon was out of breath blurted—"He was caught for robbery at the diner. Turn the TV on", yelled Samuel.

She listened and quickly ran towards the television and right before her eyes she could not believe what she was watching. The boy she loved was now under arrest. You can hear the reporter in the television—"we now caught the bandits who thought they could get away with several robberies. But it all failed and now the community can now breathe a sigh of relief and now sleep'. "And would you believe' said the reporter as she continued—they even arrested one of robbers who was also—as she air quotes "the shooter" at the Winslow high school.

Nia could not believe her eyes and ears from what she was hearing and watching.

As she watched the drama unravel on television, she spotted Robin. Then the camera focused on him. Once finding out he was the "shooter". He was handcuffed and shackled on both legs.

Robin looked up at the television and mouthed "I love you, I'm sorry". Nia dropped herself to the floor weeping in disbelief. Samuel consoled Nia as she cried—"oh Samuel—I'm so stupid, I'm so stupid why didn't I see it" she then looked at Samuel and said—you know Natalie and Sophia told me, but I just did not want to see it.

"Nia, said Samuel, handing her a box of tissues, it happens to the best of us. Is better now than later, don't you think?" 'Or when you may have been married or with children".

"But" said Nia as she sobbed, 'the thing is Samuel, I still love him, he was a different person when he was around me" as she wiped her tears. "Think Nia what your life would have been"— Samuel reassured her as they hugged.

"Nia your young and beautiful and intelligent. You have a life ahead of you. Go enjoy your youth, enjoy your life and soar!" Upon hearing this from Samuel, Nia smiled and responded, "I will take it." "Thank you". They then hugged. Nia looked at Samuel and Tracey with gratitude. She thanked them both for not letting their parents know. "You both kept your end of the deal, and I thank you dearly for keeping it. I'm just so glad they didn't find out. They were clueless—she laughed faintly.

Samuel, Nia Tracey, dinners ready come and eat. They went downstairs to eat. As they all sat around the table. Ms. Mullins began to bless the food. And they began to eat their meals, Nia looked around at each one of her family members. Samuel winked and smiled at Nia as if to say it is alright as he passed the mashed potatoes.

Nia smiled in return, feeling grateful for having such a wonderful family. But her heart was aching. She knew as time passed it would heal. She then thanked the Lord above.

Closing comments:

I am grateful for the opportunity to develop my courage in writing stories. I have always wanted to write. As a matter of fact, it has been one my bucket list. I now pat myself on the back and say, I did it. It has taken me this long because I never gave myself the time. I just kept contemplating, wavering when and if.

But I now have the time since retiring. I find that after writing my first story book I will continue writing. More so especially since seeing it with my own eyes' fruition. And with Gods will anything is possible—and the time was right now. This is my time!

It is my almighty who provided the will power to pursue my dream. I'm grateful to my wonderful family and closest friends, whose encouragement and support have always motivated me. I was honored to share my exciting news with them. Thank you all dearly and I love you all!

*God is never late. He is always on time

—2 Peter 3:8